With thanks to Francine and Michel for their enthusiasm
and for their kind participation in this book.

THIS IS A NEW YORK REVIEW BOOK
PUBLISHED BY THE NEW YORK REVIEW OF BOOKS
435 Hudson Street, New York, NY 10014
www.nyrb.com

Originally published in France by l'école des loisirs, Paris, as
Le Prince Tigre

Library of Congress Cataloging-in-Publication Data

Names: Chen, Jiang Hong, 1963– author, illustrator. | Waters, Alyson, 1955– translator.
Title: The tiger prince / by Chen Jiang Hong ; translated by Alyson Waters.
Other titles: Prince Tigre. English
Description: New York : New York Review Books, [2018] | Series: New York
Review children's collection | Summary: When a tigress whose cubs were
killed by hunters ravages villages, the king gathers his army but Lao Lao,
a seer, advises him to send his son, Wen, to the tiger, instead.
Identifiers: LCCN 2018010216 (print) | LCCN 2018017549 (ebook)
| ISBN 9781681372952 (epub) | ISBN 9781681372945 (hardback)
Subjects: | CYAC: Kings, queens, rulers, etc.—Fiction. | Princes—Fiction. |
Tigers—Fiction. | Oracles—Fiction. | China—Fiction. | BISAC: JUVENILE
FICTION / Animals / Lions, Tigers, Leopards, etc.. |
JUVENILE FICTION / Fairy Tales & Folklore / Country & Ethnic.
| JUVENILE FICTION / Action Adventure / General.
Classification: LCC PZ7.C418155 (ebook) |
LCC PZ7.C418155 Tig 2018 (print) | DDC [E]—dc23
LC record available at https://lccn.loc.gov/2018010216

ISBN 978-1-68137-294-5

Manufactured in China
Printed on acid-free paper.
2 4 6 8 10 9 7 5 3 1

Chen Jiang Hong

The Tiger Prince

Translated from the French
by Alyson Waters

The New York Review Children's Collection
New York

Deep in the great forest, the Tigress is mourning the death of her cubs. Hunters came and killed them. She couldn't save them. Ever since, she's been pacing back and forth, prowling around the villages, her heart filled with sadness and hatred.

One evening, she attacks. She destroys houses, devours people and beasts alike, but her anger does not let up. Not at all. The next day she attacks another village, and then another. When night falls, all you can hear are cries of terror everywhere.

The King has already called up his army. He questions the old woman Lao Lao, who can predict the future by tossing pebbles and bamboo sticks.

"Don't send out the army, Your Majesty," she says. "This will make the Tigress even more fearsome. Only one thing can appease her in her fury. You must give her your son, Wen."

"Sacrifice my son?" cries the King.

"I promise, Your Majesty, no harm will come to him."

The King and Queen are brokenhearted.
Wen, however, seems neither sad nor frightened.
When he gets out of his warm bath,
his small bundle is ready.

The Queen gives him
a piece of jade to protect him.
"Wherever you go, my child,
I will be with you!"

When day breaks, the King brings Wen to the edge of the great forest. "Now you must go on alone. The Tigress's territory is on the other side of this bridge. Don't be afraid. No harm will come to you."

"I'm not afraid," Wen replies.
He crosses the bridge, and disappears into the forest.

Wen walks for a long time.
Then, exhausted, he falls asleep under a tree.

The Tigress can smell him.

She draws near....

Just as she's about to attack,
instinct overcomes her.
She takes Wen in her mouth
the way she used to take her cubs.
And suddenly, all of her anger vanishes.

Very gently, the Tigress places Wen back on the ground…

...and lies down beside him to keep him warm.

"Are you hungry?" she asks Wen as soon as he wakes up, offering him the food he brought in his little bundle.

"Do you know how to dance the royal drum dance?" asks Wen.

The Tigress doesn't answer but guides him across the mountain until they come to the entrance of a cave.

The cave is a passageway…

...that leads to the heart of the Tigress's territory. Wen is filled with awe.

One day, while the Tigress is napping, Wen finds the tip of an arrow stuck in her pelt. She rears up and roars.
The memory of her wound reignites her anger.

She looks like she's
about to devour Wen.

But then Wen's frightened eyes remind her of the eyes of her cubs. Her motherly love returns.

And ever so gently,
she takes Wen in her mouth
to comfort him.

The Tigress never attacks the villages again.
She watches over Wen night and day, and teaches
him everything a little tiger needs to know.
The seasons pass and Wen grows up.
Soon the forest holds no more secrets for him.

But back in the palace, the King and Queen are terribly sad. They wonder if their son is still alive. One day, the King can't take it anymore. He sends in his army.

The soldiers spread out through the forest…

…lighting fires.

Wen and the Tigress are trapped.

Wen throws himself in front of the Tigress to protect her.
"Don't shoot!" he cries. "Back away!"

Suddenly a woman's voice can be heard: "Let me pass!"
It's the Queen. She moves through the ranks of soldiers and runs toward her son.
Wen immediately recognizes his mother's face.

"Tigress," he says, "this is my other mother. You are my two mothers, the one from the forest and the one from the palace. Now I have to return to the palace to learn what princes know. But I will come back often, because I don't want to forget what tigers know."

The Tigress slowly walks away and disappears into the forest.

Every year, Wen comes back to visit the Tigress, who waits for him at the cave's entrance. And then, one day, he comes with a tiny child. "This is my son," he says. "Keep him with you as long as it takes to teach him everything that a tiger needs to know. And then he can become a prince."

This story was inspired by a bronze vessel from the eleventh century BC, at the end of the Shang dynasty. A vessel of this kind was called a "You." This particular one, known as *The Tigress*, is held in the Cernuschi Museum in Paris. It refers to a Chinese folktale about a child named Ziwen who as a baby was taken in by a tigress.